Scrapbooks of America™

Published by Tradition Books® and distributed to the school and library market by The Child's World®
P.O. Box 326, Chanhassen, MN 55317-0326 ➤ 800/599-READ ➤ *http://www.childsworld.com*

Photo Credits: Cover: Underwood & Underwood/Corbis; Lucien Aigner/Corbis: 16, 18; Bettmann/Corbis: 6, 7, 9, 13, 15, 22, 24, 28, 31, 38, 40; Corbis: 10, 12, 39; Lois Ellen Frank/Corbis: 35; Royalty-Free/Corbis: 32; Underwood & Underwood/Corbis: 17, 23, 37

An Editorial Directions book
Editorial Directions, Inc.: E. Russell Primm, Editorial Director; Lucia Raatma, Line Editor, Photo Selector, and Additional Writing; Katie Marsico, Assistant Editor; Olivia Nellums, Editorial Assistant; Susan Hindman, Copy Editor; Susan Ashley, Proofreader; Alice Flanagan, Photo Researcher and Additional Writer

Design: The Design Lab

Library of Congress Cataloging-in-Publication Data
Dell, Pamela.
  Shaky Bones : a story of the Harlem Renaissance / by Pamela J. Dell.
     p. cm. — (Scrapbooks of America)
"An Editorial Directions book."
Summary: In 1926, a twelve-year-old aspiring poet nicknamed Shaky Bones enters the first annual Harlem All-School Young Poets Competition.
  ISBN 1-59187-040-2 (library bound : alk. paper)
  1. Harlem Renaissance—Juvenile fiction. 2. African Americans—Juvenile fiction. [1. Harlem Renaissance—Fiction. 2. African Americans—Fiction. 3. Poetry—Fiction. 4. Harlem (New York, N.Y.)—History—20th century—Fiction.] I. Title.
  PZ7.D3845 Sh 2004
  [Fic]—dc21   2003008448

Scrapbooks of America™

SHAKY BONES
A Story of the Harlem Renaissance

by Pamela Dell

TRADITION BOOKS®
A New Tradition in Children's Publishing™
MAPLE PLAIN, MINNESOTA

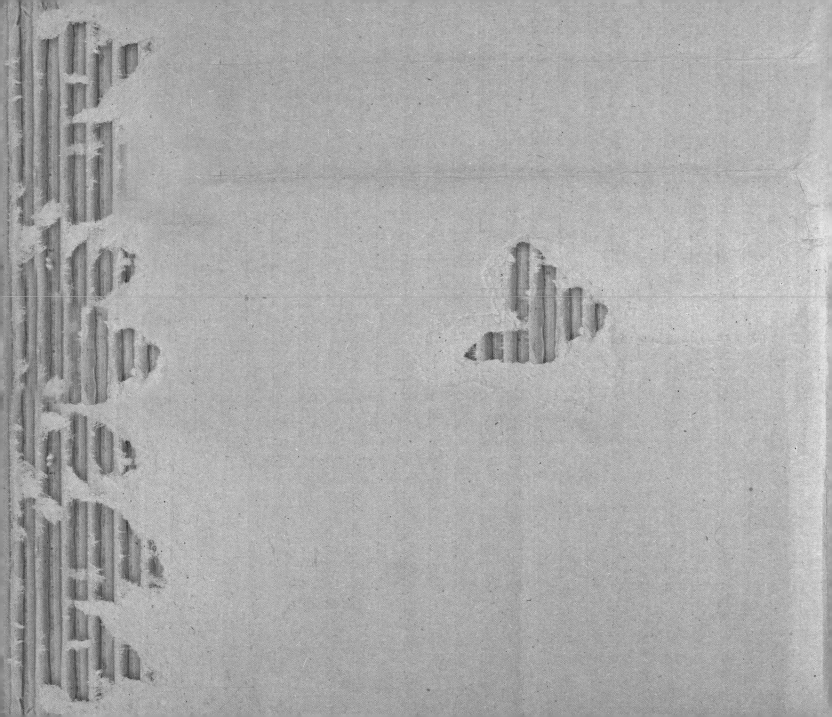

table of contents

Shaky's Story, page 6

The History of the Harlem Renaissance, page 40

Glossary, page 42

Timeline, page 42

Activities, page 44

To Find Out More, page 46

About the Author, page 48

"**Hey!** Shaky Bones! How's it going?"
One of two old guys playing checkers near the corner of 137th Street and Lenox Avenue called out to me as I came toward them. It was a crisp November Saturday, and the streets of Harlem were buzzing and popping with activity.

"Good," I said. "Real good."

Behind them, inside the barber shop, I could hear Ethel Waters singing "Midnight Blues" on the radio. Just hearing that tune set my shoulders swaying and my fingers snapping.

"There he goes," one said to the other. He made a move with his red piece on the checkerboard.

6

In addition to playing checkers, old men on the streets of Harlem used to tell Hoodoo stories. Hoodoo is the American version of voodoo, a belief in magic and spells that is common in Haiti.

Throughout Harlem, men gathered to talk and play checkers.

Harlem was a busy and wonderful place—filled with people and cars, music and art.

"Shake those bones, boy," the second one added, looking up at me. They both chuckled. I didn't mind. Music loved me, and I sure loved it.

"You planning on entering that poetry competition come Thanksgiving?" the first guy asked.

"Don't know about that yet," I replied. But I did know. And I couldn't stop to chat. I was on my way to the Temple of All Knowledge, as I liked to call it. Everybody else just knew it as the 135th Street Public Library, but to me it was nearly the best place in that whole north end of New York City. A place to find out all you might ever need or want to know. Things to open doors. Things to give you power. Things to make you laugh.

That's why I spent as much time there as I could. Figured I needed all those things, and more.

"Keep shaking those bones!" one of the old men called after me as I passed, leaving them to their game. I heard their laughter rise behind me, and I chuckled with enjoyment myself.

As I turned onto bustling Lenox Avenue, I was still feeling the music and it felt good. Seemed I'd had **rhythm** rocking my bones ever since I'd been born. Music—**jazz** and **spirituals** and **blues**—all of it swarmed those streets, jump-starting me inside and out. You could hear it anyplace your footsteps took you in Harlem, and it kept me bouncing day and night as I ran the errands, took the messages, made the deliveries from one address to another.

At night, those shiny brass horns like my daddy played would blare from every club along 133rd Street, and from plenty of other, more private places, too. Always a sweet piano, the snaky weave of **reed instruments,** and the drums that got my head bobbing and my fingers beating against my thigh bone. All the pieces wove together, making magic. I couldn't keep still!

The music moved in my mind, too. It stormed from my brain right down my arm

The Harlem Renaissance was an exciting and creative time. African-American artists, writers, and musicians in New York and throughout the country produced amazing work during this period, primarily in the 1920s.

Reeds are part of a band's woodwind section. When a player blows over the reed in the mouthpiece of one of these instruments, it vibrates and makes a great sound.

People all over Harlem enjoyed the music of entertainers like these at Small's Paradise Club.

and into my pencil, till it flooded out onto the page in words. Poetry words.

I aimed to be a fine poet, like Countee Cullen or Langston Hughes or one of those other great **Negro** word masters I knew were publishing books and winning awards. Maybe I'd never make it that good, good as they did, but I was working on it. Doing my best.

Reading and writing poetry moved me as much as music did. I wanted to string words together like song beads to make poems. Music words. Words that jumped and jammed.

Jingling, jangling, jamming, juicing, jumping words!

I'd string those J-words together in my mind and feel the energy of them jazz my

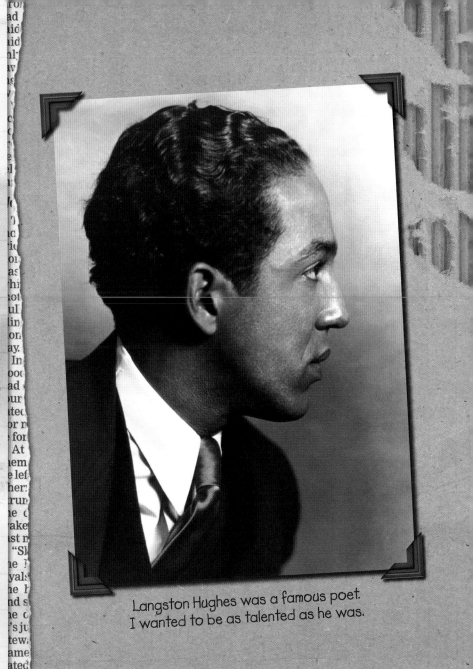

Langston Hughes was a famous poet. I wanted to be as talented as he was.

soul. Then I'd say them out loud. Shout them sometimes, even. The faster you could say those words all together, I discovered, the more energy you got moving through your body. It was a good chant to get the music juices flowing and your bones shaking. Shaking bones—that felt good.

It was two years earlier, in 1924, that someone hung the name Shaky Bones on me. In March of that year, I turned ten and my daddy's band got a job playing at a special celebration put on at the Civic Club. It was a fine and fancy dinner to honor Jessie Fauset for the publication of her first novel. She was one of a whole bunch of what my daddy called bright young stars who were going to be at that dinner. Young Negro writers who were beginning to make people everywhere look up and take serious notice.

Writers were leading the way, moving into the **limelight** by turning their words into a powerful art. But plenty more artists of every kind were coming right along with them and getting attention, too. Painters and photographers, musicians and singers. Even dress designers like my mama, who had her very own shop.

In our little end part of New York, you could almost hear the pop and fizz of creativity exploding. Daddy and Mama

A huge number of African-Americans moved to northern cities (such as New York and Chicago) around the time of World War I (1914-1918). Their presence in New York was one reason that the Harlem Renaissance happened.

taught us to recognize it, all that creative juice and deep thinking brought together there in Harlem. All kinds of thinking people spreading powerful new thoughts to folks, black and white both, all over the whole country. Maybe even the whole world, I hoped. Thoughts that, along with all the fine art, were showing the world how much beauty and power were living a fiery life inside our people. Jessie Fauset was one of those helping to make that happen.

I knew of Jessie Fauset for another reason, too. It was because she had published a six-line poem of mine when I was only seven. I'd sent it to the *Brownies' Book* and, as the editor there, she'd chosen it to appear in one of the last issues that magazine ever put

Jessie Fauset was the editor of the *Brownies' Book*. She helped a lot of writers during the Harlem Renaissance.

The *Brownies' Book* magazine sold for 15 cents a copy and was produced monthly. It contained short stories, poems, and news items, mostly for African-American children.

Poet Countee Cullen was among a number of writers and other artists at the Civic Club dinner.

out. Thanks to Jessie Fauset, I could already tell folks I was a published writer.

Every single one in my family had been so excited over me getting something in a well-known children's magazine that they couldn't sit still or be quiet either. My mama had even called me a **prodigy.**

"Prodigy? What's that?" I'd asked, thinking she was making fun and meaning I was some donkey with too much pride. But she'd explained how it meant having a lot of talent in something at an early age. I was glad my family truly thought so highly of me. I liked that feeling. I wanted to keep it going. Being a poet seemed to be my way.

So a few years later, at that Civic Club dinner, I felt lucky beyond words just to be sitting under those glittery **chandeliers** in a room full of poets and other writers. I'd brought a nice autograph book just for the occasion, too. It even had my initials— S. B.—stitched into the leather cover, and my plan was to get every shining star I could to sign their name in my book. I wasn't doing too badly at it either.

After a bit, I got up my nerve and approached what seemed like the most dazzling set of stars in the whole place. There they were, Jessie Fauset and Countee Cullen themselves, conversing with W. E. B. DuBois and Charles S. Johnson, who had arranged the whole affair. I was speechless while my book circulated among them, but

Jessie Fauset's first novel was titled *There Is Confusion.*

I could feel the music working on me. It started down my legs, getting a little dance step going in my feet. My arms tingled with sound, and I shook them a bit to let the energy out.

"S. B.," Countee Cullen said. "What does that stand for, son?"

"Simon Brocade, sir," I replied. I started nodding my head to the drum beat, couldn't help it.

"I'd have thought it stood for . . ." Countee chuckled, his eyes twinkling. "Shaky Bones!" There was a whoop of laughter all around. It even made me laugh. I liked the sound of that meaning.

"Shaky Bones!" Jessie Fauset exclaimed with delight. I'd already told her all about

W. E. B. DuBois was editor of *The Crisis*. He was an important man throughout the Harlem Renaissance and for many years to come.

how she'd published my very first real poem a few years before. "I discovered Shaky Bones!"

That name spread all around that room so fast that by the time Daddy came down from playing his first set, even he had already heard it. He took it home with us that night and it spread straight through my family, too. Next thing I knew, it was all over the neighborhood, all over Harlem, and that was it. Shaky Bones, young poet of the New Negro Movement, had been born.

———

So that November morning two and a half years later, I entered the Temple of

All Knowledge with a mission in mind.
It was not only a place to learn fantastic
things—it was also a quiet hideaway
to work on my poetry with nobody to
bother me.

"Hello!" I said to Miss Anderson, the
assistant librarian, as I came in to the library.
Furthering the arts was something she cared
about a lot. It had even been her idea to
organize the students' poetry competition,
which was to be held the Wednesday evening
before Thanksgiving.

I hadn't shown a single soul what I was
working on, but from the minute she knew
I planned to enter the competition, Miss
Anderson had encouraged me. Not only had
she introduced me to books of poetry, but

The library was a great place for lots of us to study and
read. I loved spending time there.

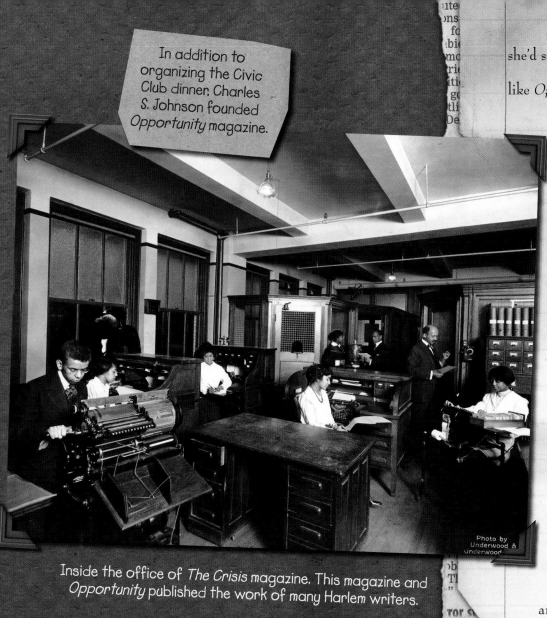

In addition to organizing the Civic Club dinner, Charles S. Johnson founded *Opportunity* magazine.

Inside the office of *The Crisis* magazine. This magazine and *Opportunity* published the work of many Harlem writers.

she'd saved clippings for me from magazines like *Opportunity* and *The Crisis*. These clippings were of new poems by famous writers, or they talked about the accomplishments of other young Negro men and women, which gave me the kind of courage I needed to keep on trying such things myself.

I planned to get up there onstage at that competition and read my poem out in front of the judges. I meant to make everybody's hair stand on end with how good my piece would sound when I read it aloud like that.

I sat down at a library table and opened my cardboard folder full of papers. I had a lot of papers with scribbles of first, second, and third tries on them. I was getting there but it wasn't all together yet. I still had a few weeks until Thanksgiving, though, so I wasn't too worried.

I was hard at work on my poem when I heard a kind of snorting sound. I didn't look up right away, but I was already dreading what I was about to see. I knew that sound. It was the Blob.

I knew he'd be heading right my way, but before I could say a word to stop him, he sat down at the very same library table I was seated at. Disgusted, I crumpled another bad version of my poem and pitched it in the nearby trash can. The can was filled with paper snowballs, all different crumpled up

Lots of kids used the library. But sometimes I pretended I had it all to myself.

attempts I'd made to get the lines just right. It was supposed to be about freedom-making music, and some of those lines were working just fine. But others were still giving me trouble. Now with the Blob at my table, I was convinced it was going to be even more trouble.

Finally I looked up at him. At least he'd had enough sense to sit on the other side of the table from me, and down at the other end.

"Hi, Shaky," he said.

"Hello, Lester," I answered. Without another word, I turned my eyes back down to my papers. I deliberately rewrote a line, pretending I was still alone. I needed to show him I was busy. Very, very busy.

The Blob made another snuffly, snorting sound, and I couldn't help myself. I stared back up at him, irritated. He looked like a big toasty cream puff with two dark eyes stuck in it like a couple of chocolate drops. But it wasn't so much his size or his shape that made me think of him as a blob. It was really because there wasn't a single thing about him that was his own.

"The boy got no personality at all!" I'd complained to Mama when I first began to notice it. "Just a dang blob who imitates everything I do! Blob who wants to *be* me, it seems!"

"Now be kind," my mama advised. "That boy is paying you a **compliment** by that be-havior of his."

"If that's true, it's a compliment I don't

want!" I was feeling scratchy and twitchy just thinking about it. I was getting all jangly in my nerves.

Mama gave me that look of hers, like I should be ashamed to talk so. But I'd worked myself up about it good by then and couldn't stop.

"If I come to school with a new pair of shoes, or a fine new pen, sure enough, the Blob's got something just like it the very next day," I told her, hoping to justify myself in her eyes. "Or I get the buzz going about me wanting messenger and delivery work after school, and all the clubs start picking up on that, giving me jobs. Next thing I know, the Blob's going around asking if he might get delivery duties himself. At all those same places! It just keeps going on like that, all the time!"

"His imitating you that way just means he admires you and wants to be like you himself," Mama pointed out, all calm and reasonable.

"But he's not me!" I bellowed, fed up. "He's not me and he's sure not his own self either! He's nothing but a big blob of nobody!"

"Now, Simon, don't you be talking like that about another human being!" Mama scolded. "You know you wouldn't want anyone talking that way about you, so don't you give what you don't want to get."

In 1926, the Carnegie Corporation helped the 135th Street Public Library buy Arturo Schomburg's vast collection of art reflecting African-American culture throughout the world. These materials became the basis for the Schomburg Center for Research in Black Culture.

Mama was right, of course, but it was just darn difficult to ease up on Lester. Especially when there he was, talking at me in the hush of the library, a place not meant for useless socializing and chatter.

From my spot at the opposite end of the table, his snuffle rose again to my ears.

"What you working on?" he asked.

I raised my head and met his eyes square on. "I'll be working on you right fine if you don't leave off my business!" I replied.

"Jeez, Shaky," he said. "I didn't mean any offense. Just wondering, that's all."

"Well, you can just quit wondering, Lester!" He made me so mad I found myself slamming my folder shut and pushing back my chair with a loud screech. The next second I was taking off for the book stacks. I *did* feel ashamed of myself for being so harsh on him, but enough was enough!

I spent several minutes fuming in the stacks. While I hunted through the poetry books, I could barely keep my mind off the Blob. The only good thing I could find about him was that we were in all different classes that year. When I felt I'd cooled down enough to face him again, I came back to the table. But right away, I noticed he had a grip on the corner of my folder and was peeking inside. He saw me and instantly pulled his hand away and turned his head down to his own stuff.

"Lester," I hissed, "what are you doing now? Why you always got to be in my business?!" I scooped up my folder, tucked my books under my arm, ready to go sit some-place else.

"I wasn't doing anything!" he whined. "Just looking for a blank sheet of paper, Shaky!" He got to his feet, too.

"Uh-huh," I said, watching him with my mind all full of suspicion.

"Never mind," the Blob said. "Guess I know when I'm not wanted. I'll see you, big Mr. Shaky Bones."

I watched silently as Lester bumbled his way toward the exit as quick as he could, not once looking back. Then I settled down and, finally content, continued the work on my **masterpiece.**

All through November I spent every

The great African-American poet Langston Hughes used the rhythms of music, including jazz and the blues, in many of his poems.

I hoped my poetry had the same kind of rhythm that people danced to in Harlem nightclubs.

The Cotton Club was a well-known nightspot in Harlem. Some of the finest musicians of the 1920s played on its stage.

spare minute whipping my music-power poem into shape. I wrote and rewrote, polished and practiced. By the big night, I felt pretty confident about taking the stage to perform.

Confident terror, more like. My daddy might stand up on a stage and do a blazing trumpet solo every night in this neighborhood. My mama might get written about and photographed by the famous James Van der Zee, right alongside elegant young ladies in the beautiful gowns she created. But I wasn't used to that kind of limelight. Still, Daddy, Mama, and the whole rest of my family were going to be there watching and I had to do right by them.

The Lafayette Theatre, where the Harlem All-School Young Poets Competition took place

I could hardly believe our performance was going to be in a real theater. The Lafayette Theatre had donated the space from 4:30 until 6:30, well before that night's regular show. There was a set of audience seats blocked off for all the performers, so that after we'd read our work, we could sit out front and at the end watch the awards being given.

From backstage I could hear the **murmuring** crowd as they filed in. I stole a peek out from behind the curtain. The place was filling up with families and friends and anyone else brave enough to **witness** the first annual Harlem All-School Young Poets Competition, as it was being called. The first row on the left side had five seats reserved for the judges, and they were all already seated. But the only ones I recognized were Countee Cullen and Mrs. Handy, whom I knew to be the Blob's English teacher. Looking their way, I felt my heart start slamming somewhat and I retreated into the way-back part of backstage to be alone for a few minutes. I needed to do one more practice run before it was my turn to go on.

I was number fourteen in the junior high division, so I thought I'd be waiting a while until I was up. But once the whole thing got started, it seemed like time went crazy on me.

The Lafayette Theatre, also known as the "House Beautiful," was located at 132nd Street and 7th Avenue. It was one of the first theaters to allow blacks and whites in the audience together.

Before I knew it, the **master of ceremonies** was calling my name from out front.

"And now," she said, "we'll hear from seventh-grader Simon Brocade!" I heard an eruption of hoots and hollers and applause as I pushed my way out from behind the curtain. It seemed every darned relative I'd ever owned must be out there in the audience, along with a heap of friends.

I made it to center stage without tripping, a thing I'd been fearing all along. I looked out into the darkness in front of me. The bright lights on my face kept me from seeing most everyone too clearly, and I was glad about that. I was up, no turning back.

"My poem," I began, "is called 'Shaky Bones.'"

A total hush seemed to fall on the audience. It was so quiet I feared everyone there could hear my heart tick-tocking behind my ribs. Had to go, had to keep on.

"Jinglin', janglin', jammin', juicin', jumpin'!" I began. Then I rushed on:

"That music man,

"He reaches down with both hands,

"Pulls it on up, right out of me.

"Won't stop till it's right on top,

"That bone-shakin', soul-breakin'

"Rhythm, rhyme, and blues beat.

"Powers me up from inside out,

"Till I got to move, got to shout.

"Got the beat,

"Feel the heat,

"I'm powered up with the jammin' jive,

"Deep feeling, every inch of me

wide-alive!

"Here it comes,

"Jinglin', janglin', jammin', juicin', jumpin'

from deep inside!

"Shakin', shakin' my bones."

I caught my breath.

"Now say those J-words!" I finished.

I was only a little surprised when a few people in the audience called the whole string right back to me.

"Again!" I commanded. "Jinglin', janglin', jammin', juicin', jumpin'!" This time it came louder, more folks joined in. I felt good. I felt strong. I was clearing the finish line, and I knew I hadn't done too bad.

"One last time!" Now the whole audi-ence was right along with me—I could feel it. I raised my arms high over my head, shaking my wrists, and we chanted all together. "Jinglin', janglin', jammin', juicin', jumpin'!"

That was it, my whole poem out there. I dropped my arms.

There was a long pause, while the audi-ence made sure I was really finished, and then it was like a crazy uproar took over that place. People up on their feet applaud-ing. Even a series of long, high-pitched whistles from different corners of the theater. I bowed at the waist, straightened up, and rushed offstage, all that **ruckus** tailing me as I went.

A lot of people from my school came to the poetry competition.
It was exciting to see them all in the crowd.

After our whole junior high division had performed, I felt sure I'd be right up there somewhere on top. There were some good poets who'd read, but still I figured I might be able to get at least second prize.

From the side section we were now seated in, I could see the judges looking at their notes and huddling together whispering. Somebody in the audience cried out, "Shaky's got it!" followed by a short blast of further hollers. I looked down at my hands, placed firmly on my knees just in case my bones started to bounce around a little too much. *Come on!* I thought. *Let's get on with it now!*

Finally, one of the judges made his way to the stage. More cheering. I heard the names of various kids who'd read being called out from the audience. Then the judge spoke.

"Good evening, ladies and gentlemen," he began. "This is a proud day for all our young people who aspire to become great men and women of the poetic word. For an artist, the creation of those words is a mysterious and original act. No two can ever come up with exactly the same set of words. So I regret to inform this audience now that one of the works read here tonight is a **plagiarism** and must be **disqualified.**"

He turned slightly and looked toward us. I glanced around, wondering who it was who'd had the nerve to steal someone else's writing and call it their own.

"Unfortunately," the judge said, "on

these grounds, we have to disqualify—Simon Brocade."

"What?!" I screamed, standing bolt upright at the very same moment the entire audience seemed to go suddenly crazy. Over the **hubbub**, I tried to be heard.

"That's *my* poem!" I hollered. "I didn't thieve from anybody! I worked that whole thing out myself!"

The judge was calling for quiet. The audience settled somewhat, but mostly they were still chattering madly and looking my way. No way was I going to hang around for the rest of the outrage. I stormed off just as Mrs. Handy came onstage to stand beside the other judge.

"People!" I heard her say as I made my way up the aisle toward the exit. I felt my face in a fury and it seemed as if dark funnels of smoke were shooting from my ears. "It's my duty to let you know that one of my own pupils wrote a poem nearly identical to the one in question. He read it in class several weeks ago. The true author of that poem is Lester Faircloth!"

Lester Faircloth?! The Blob?! *Oh no. Oh no-no-NO you don't, Lester Faircloth!* I thought as I pushed out of that theater and onto Seventh Avenue. Somewhere in that mess behind, my family was no doubt feeling badly shamed, but I couldn't wait around to explain it to them right then. I had to go straight to the root of the problem. And I knew just where that root was at this hour: his **clarinet** lesson.

Trumpeteer Louis Armstrong playing with his band. Both Lester and I wished we could play like they did.

The music of Harlem was made with all sorts of instruments and by all kinds of people.

Ever since the Blob had discovered my daddy was teaching me how to blow a **saxophone,** he'd suddenly been telling the world all about his own Wednesday evening clarinet lessons. And I knew where his teacher, Bo Brady, lived, as he just so happened to be a friend of my parents.

In only a few minutes, there I was pounding on Bo's door. It was dark and chilly outside, and in the streets, one sleek and shiny car after another was passing by. Inside those cars, I knew, were ladies in furs, gentlemen in top hats, just starting their night on the town.

I pounded again.

When Bo finally let me in, I went straight for Lester, who was standing back in the parlor.

"Fool, what's wrong with you?!" I shouted. Lester backed up a step, looking confused.

Bo came up behind me.

"Shaky!" he said, "Settle down. What's the problem?"

I ignored him. Didn't want to, but I needed to get my words out on the Blob before a vein in my neck burst from holding it in.

"What?" Lester said, beginning to look fearful.

"What do you mean, *'what'*?! You crazy? That's plagiarism you tried to get away with, Lester!" I felt I had to spell it out for him. "P-L-A-G-I-A-R-I-S-M! That's a big word and an even bigger problem, fool!"

"Hey, ease up, Shaky!" Bo said, getting

in between Lester and me. "And I don't want you calling anyone 'fool' in my house, you hear me? Now, what's this plagiarism stuff?"

I spilled the whole story in about two seconds, mostly at the top of my lungs. The whole while, Lester was standing close beside Bo, as if he felt more protected that way. But his face was plastered with a sad, **sheepish** look that kept me angry just looking at it.

With Bo as calm as he was, I did begin to cool off a **smidgen.** Then, bit by bit, Lester's side came out. It seemed Mrs. Handy had assigned her class to write a poem to read aloud. But, Lester admitted, not being all that poetic, he felt he had to do something to make do. And that something turned out to be slipping a page from my folder that day in the library.

"I figured, who'd ever know?" he confessed. "It was just one little poem, and just inside my class, nowhere else." His voice was doing that whiny thing again.

"Shoot!" I said, the minute he finished his explanation. I turned to Bo. "I've got to get, Bo. Lester's ruined my whole night, and even worse, he made my family look bad. I need to go fix all that."

"I understand," Bo said, looking from me to the Blob. "I think Lester needs to fix a few things himself."

Last I saw of him, Lester was wearing that mournful look on his cream-puff face, chocolate-drop eyes not daring to even look at me. Then I was out of there.

Traditional Thanksgiving food for African-Americans during this time might include roasted pumpkin seeds, African chicken stew, baked sweet potatoes with ginger and honey, grilled curried vegetables, grilled oysters, and peanut pie.

We had a great Thanksgiving that year, even if Lester had ruined my performance at the poetry contest.

Back home and considerably calmed down, I explained the whole situation to my family. I was still plenty upset that the entire world was thinking I was the one who did wrong, but that didn't keep me from stuffing my guts with turkey and all the trimmings at dinner the next afternoon.

"Just remember, Shaky," my daddy advised after we'd bowed our heads and said **grace,** "you got the talent. Be grateful for that and be glad you're not so desperate you need to be dishonest in this world. And don't you worry, son. The truth about what happened last night will get around, believe me."

"That's right," Mama agreed. "You didn't do a thing wrong, so you can hold your head up even if the whole world thinks otherwise."

All the rest of my relatives around the Thanksgiving table nodded and chimed in agreeing.

———

Not long after that, a small piece appeared in *The Crisis*, summing up the events surrounding the first annual Harlem All-School Young Poets Competition. It told all about how the poem titled "Shaky Bones" was an original work by Simon Brocade of 137th Street. It told how, weeks before, Miss Regina Anderson, assistant librarian, had discovered several earlier drafts of the work in a library trash can, which served as proof. And finally, it mentioned that the person who had claimed the poem as his own had confessed and apologized to all the proper parties. Further, that person was deeply sorry about the mistake and, to make up for it, had been given the job of working after school cleaning chalkboards until winter vacation. With no pay.

Reading that, I felt a little bit sorry for the Blob. Lester, I mean. He still had to take responsibility for his crime, of course. But I figured if you don't learn to forgive a person who's done you wrong, you turn into stone outside and start to rot inside. I wanted to be someone who, when people looked at me going by, they'd say, "Look! There goes Shaky Bones! Now that's one **righteous** man worth knowing. He's got talent. He's got smarts. But even better than that, he's carrying a big fine heart full of wisdom."

Regina Andrews (whose maiden name was Anderson) loved her work at the library and she encouraged many young writers. Under the name Ursala Tilling, she wrote a play called *Climbing Jacob's Ladder.*

The 1920s were an interesting time in Harlem, and we were proud to call that neighborhood our home.

In December I stayed late one evening after school to talk over my new piece of poetry with my teacher. On the way out of the school, I saw Lester finishing up his chalkboard chores.

"Hey, Lester," I said. "You want to go get a hot chocolate and a cinnamon bun?"

He looked at me, shocked, I could tell. "With you?" he said, unbelieving.

"Yeah, man," I replied. "I'll buy, too."

See, I was feeling generous. Not only did I have a small heap of cash saved up from all my jobs, but I had a brand-new ten-dollar bill and a blue ribbon for winning first prize in the junior high division of the poetry competition.

Yep, that's how it turned out after all the

The first issue of *The Crisis*, the magazine that later carried a notice about the poetry competition

James Van der Zee was considered to be the most important portrait photographer in Harlem. His studio, which opened in 1918, was at 272 Lenox Avenue.

A Harlem dancer, photographed by James Van Der Zee, a well-respected photographer during the Renaissance

fuss was cleared up. There it was: First Prize to Mr. Simon Brocade for his poem "Shaky Bones."

Just the thought of that sentence published where all could read it was still making me feel good. As I walked up Lenox Avenue with Lester in the darkening afternoon, I could hear the music all around me. The rhythm and hum of it was **vibrating** in the air, just like always. All up and down the street, lights were beginning to pop on in the stores and clubs and homes. It was almost like the music was magic, making all that lighting up happen, both on the streets and in my own soul. My head began bobbing to the beat and my shoulders started swaying. That shaky-boned feeling was a fine, fine thing. ❧

THE HISTORY OF THE
HARLEM RENAISSANCE

Twelve-year-old Simon Brocade grew up in an amazing place during an exciting time. Between 1916 and 1940, a group of talented African-American writers, artists, musicians, and actors had settled in a 2-square-mile (5-square-kilometer) area of New York City known as Harlem. Their creative talents gave birth to a unique expression of African-American culture called the Harlem Renaissance.

During this era, Harlem was a city within a city, made up of tens of thousands of African-Americans, many of whom had moved there from the South to improve their lives. Quickly the population had grown into a hard-working, educated, and professional middle class. In this unique community, a variety of stores, churches, newspapers, banks, and social clubs flourished.

New musical forms, such as the blues and jazz, also came into being. Based on slave songs and rhythms, these new kinds of music spread rapidly and changed forever the way Americans danced, sang, and played instruments. During this era, the Jazz Age was ushered in and new approaches to musical theater were introduced on Broadway. Brilliant composers and musicians, such as Duke Ellington and Eubie Blake, spearheaded the golden age of jazz and influenced great performers like singer Ethel Waters and dancer Bill "Bojangles" Robinson. Their achievements helped revolutionize the entertainment business.

When black musicals introduced new dances called the Charleston and the Black Bottom, jazz dancing became as popular as the songs that white and black people were singing in communities across America. During this creative time, African-American writers were also making their mark. The profound ideas of W. E. B. DuBois, James Weldon Johnson, and Claude McKay captured the interest of freedom-loving people everywhere and laid the groundwork for future civil rights movements in the United States. The Harlem Renaissance began in New York City in the 1920s, and its influence on art and literature continues to be appreciated throughout the world today.

GLOSSARY

blues a type of music developed by African-American artists in the late 1800s

chandeliers light fixtures that hang from the ceiling and are usually made of many small lights

clarinet a long, hollow musical instrument that is a type of wood-wind

compliment a comment that shows admiration and respect for another person

disqualified prevented from participating in a contest or other event, usually because rules have been broken

grace a short prayer of thanks said before a meal

hubbub noisy confusion

jazz a type of music that uses rhythms in interesting ways; originated by African Americans in New Orleans around 1900 to 1905

limelight the center of attention

master of ceremonies someone who acts as host at a show or public event

masterpiece an outstanding piece of work, such as art or literature; often means a person's best work

murmuring talking quietly and making a low, continuous sound

TIMELINE

1865–1868 America begins to rebuild as a nation after the Civil War, and a law is passed that guarantees African-Americans the same rights as white citizens.

1909 The National Negro Committee (later known as the National Association for the Advancement of Colored People) meets for the first time in New York City.

1910 The first copy of *The Crisis* magazine is printed.

1915–1920 Between 500,000 and 1 million southern African-Americans begin moving north in the hopes of finding work; this flow of blacks to northern states such as New York continues for many years and becomes known as the Great Migration.

1921 The last issue of the *Brownies' Book* is published in December; *Shuffle Along* opens in New York City.

Negro an old-fashioned term for African-American

plagiarism the act of stealing the words of another and using them as one's own

prodigy an extremely smart and talented child

reed instruments musical instruments, such as the clarinet, oboe, and saxophone, that have a thin piece of metal, wood, or plastic in the mouthpiece

rhythm a regular beat used in music, dance, and poetry

righteous doing what is right and following moral laws

ruckus a noisy commotion

saxophone a musical instrument that is usually made of brass and has a mouthpiece, keys, and a curved body

sheepish embarrassed or ashamed

smidgen a small amount

spirituals songs that are religious and usually emotional; originated by African-Americans in the South

vibrating moving back and forth quickly

witness to see or hear something in person

1923 Charles S. Johnson founds *Opportunity* magazine.

1924 Johnson gives a dinner at the Civic Club to honor young African-American authors such as Jessie Fauset.

1925 A special section, known as the Division of Negro History, Literature, and Prints, is opened at the 135th Street Public Library to incorporate African-American culture and art.

1926 Langston Hughes publishes *The Weary Blues,* his first book of poetry.

1929 The stock market crash in October leads to the Great Depression of the 1930s. The Harlem Renaissance begins to come to a close.

ACTIVITIES

Continuing the Story

(Writing Creatively)

Continue Shaky's story. Elaborate on an event from his scrapbook or add your own entries to the beginning or end of his journal. You might write about Shaky's relationship with Lester Faircloth or a famous author. Or you might focus on how Shaky developed his talent as a writer later in life. You can also write your own short story of historical fiction about African-American life in Harlem during the Harlem Renaissance.

Celebrating Your Heritage

(Discovering Family History)

Research your own family history. Find out if your family had any relatives living in Harlem in the 1920s and 1930s. Ask family members to write down what they know about the people and events during this time period. How were your relatives involved directly or indirectly in the Harlem Renaissance? Search for family postcards, letters, and photographs from this time period. Make drawings of family keepsakes.

Documenting History

(Exploring Community History)

Find out how your city or town was affected by the fashion, the art, the ideas, and the music and dance of the Harlem Renaissance. Visit your library, historical society, museum, or Web sites for links to the event. How did eyewitnesses describe it? What did newspapers and magazines report? When, where, why, and how did your community react to the event? Who was involved? What was the result?

Preserving Memories

(Crafting)

Make a scrapbook about African-American family life in Harlem in the 1920s. Imagine what life was like for your family or for Shaky's family. Fill the pages with special events, family stories, interviews with relatives and friends, letters, and drawings of family treasures. Add copies of newspaper and magazine articles, photos, postcards, and awards. Decorate the pages and the cover with family heirlooms, drawings of musical instruments and Shaky's poetry awards, famous authors' books, photographs of popular jazz musicians, and fashionable cars and clothing from this era.

TO FIND OUT MORE

At the Library

Beckman, Wendy Hart. *Artists and Writers of the Harlem Renaissance.*
Berkeley Heights, N.J.: Enslow, 2002.

Gaines, Ann Graham. *The Harlem Renaissance in American History.*
Berkeley Heights, N.J.: Enslow, 2002.

Raatma, Lucia. *The Harlem Renaissance: A Celebration of Creativity.*
Chanhassen, Minn.: The Child's World, 2002.

Walker, Alice. *Langston Hughes: American Poet.* New York: HarperCollins, 2002.

On the Internet

Harlem 1900–1940: An African-American Community
http://www.si.umich.edu/CHICO/Harlem
For a virtual tour of the Harlem Renaissance exhibit

Harlem Renaissance: A Portrait of Culture and Society
http://www.columbia.edu/~bjb5/erica/Harlem.html
For an overview of the arts during the renaissance

Harlem Renaissance Music
http://www.uta.edu/english/V/students/collab13/joyce.html
To learn more about music from the era

Writers of the Harlem Renaissance
http://www.readingwoman.com/harlem.html
For a sampling of writing from that period

Places to Visit

Archives of African-American Music and Culture
Indiana University
Smith Research Center
2805 E. Tenth Street
Bloomington, IN 47408
812/855-8547
To learn more about the history of African-American arts

Schomburg Center for Research in Black Culture
515 Malcolm X Boulevard
New York, NY 10037
212/491-2200
For more information about the Harlem Renaissance
and its impact on African-American culture

ABOUT THE AUTHOR

Pamela Dell has been making her living as a writer for about fifteen years. Though she has published both fiction and nonfiction for adults, in the last decade she has written mostly for kids. Her nonfiction work includes biographies, science, history, and nature topics. She has also published contemporary and historical fiction, as well as award-winning interactive multimedia. The twelve books in the Scrapbooks of America series have been some of her favorite writing projects.